JOHN JENSEN FEELS DIFFERENT

Written by Henrik Hovland Illustrated by Torill Kove

Eerdmans Books for Young Readers
Grand Rapids, Michigan • Cambridge, U.K.

Henrik Hovland is a Norwegian author and journalist. He has also worked as a war crimes investigator and a war reporter. He has written a novel and a collection of short stories, but *John Jensen Feels Different* is his first book for children. Henrik lives in Oslo.

Torill Kove is a Norwegian-born film director and animator who has also illustrated several children's books. She won an Academy Award in 2007 for her animated short film *The Danish Poet*. Torill has lived in Canada since 1982.

Original Title: Johannes Jensen føler seg annerledes
First published in Norway

Text by Henrik Hovland
Illustrations by Torill Kove

Translation by Don Bartlett

This edition published in 2012 by Eerdmans Books for Young Readers,
an imprint of Wm. B. Eerdmans Publishing Co.
2140 Oak Industrial Dr. NE
Grand Rapids, Michigan 49505
P.O. Box 163, Cambridge CB3 9PU U.K.

www.eerdmans.com/youngreaders

Manufactured at Tien Wah Press in Singapore in August 2011, first printing

19 18 17 16 15 14 13 12 9 8 7 6 5 4 3 2 1

Library of Congress Cataloging-in-Publication Data

Hovland, Henrik.
[Johannes Jensen føler seg annerledes. English]
John Jensen feels different / by Henrik Hovland; illustrated by Torill Kove; translated by Don Bartlett.
p. cm.
Summary: John Jensen, a crocodile, cannot quite understand why he feels so different from everyone else, but a kindly doctor reassures him that no one is exactly the same as anyone else.
ISBN 978-0-8028-5399-8 (alk. paper)
[1. Individuality – Fiction. 2. Crocodiles – Fiction.] I. Kove, Torill, ill. II. Title.
PZ7.H8244Jo 2012
[E] – dc23
2011022446

This translation has been published with the financial support of NORLA.

This is John Jensen.

This is where John Jensen lives.

John Jensen feels different.

He feels he's different when he eats his breakfast.

He feels he's different when he brushes his teeth.

He feels he's different when he flosses.

He feels he's different when he takes the bus to work.
John Jensen feels the other passengers are looking at him.

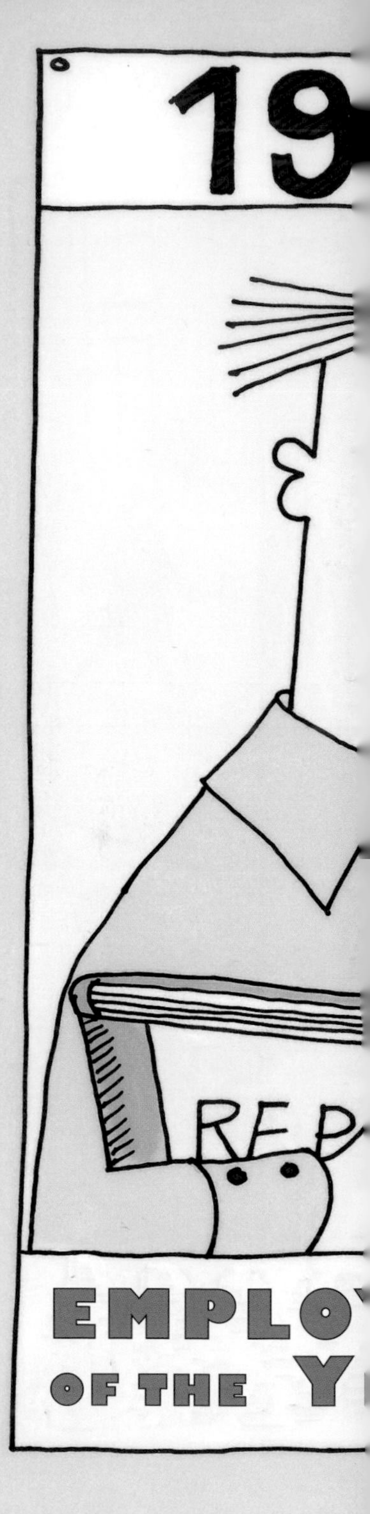

John Jensen also feels he's different when
he's sitting in the tax office working on cases.

Perhaps it's my bow tie that makes me feel different, John Jensen thinks.
No one else wears a bow tie.

The next day John Jensen wears a regular tie to work.
But he still feels he's different.

John Jensen walks home alone in the rain.

After dinner he looks in the mirror.

Maybe I was adopted, John Jensen thinks.
He doesn't seem to look like anyone else in his family.

At night he lies awake. He wonders why he feels he's different.
Perhaps it's the tail, he thinks. No one else has a tail like mine.

John Jensen decides to tie his tail to his stomach so that no one can see it.

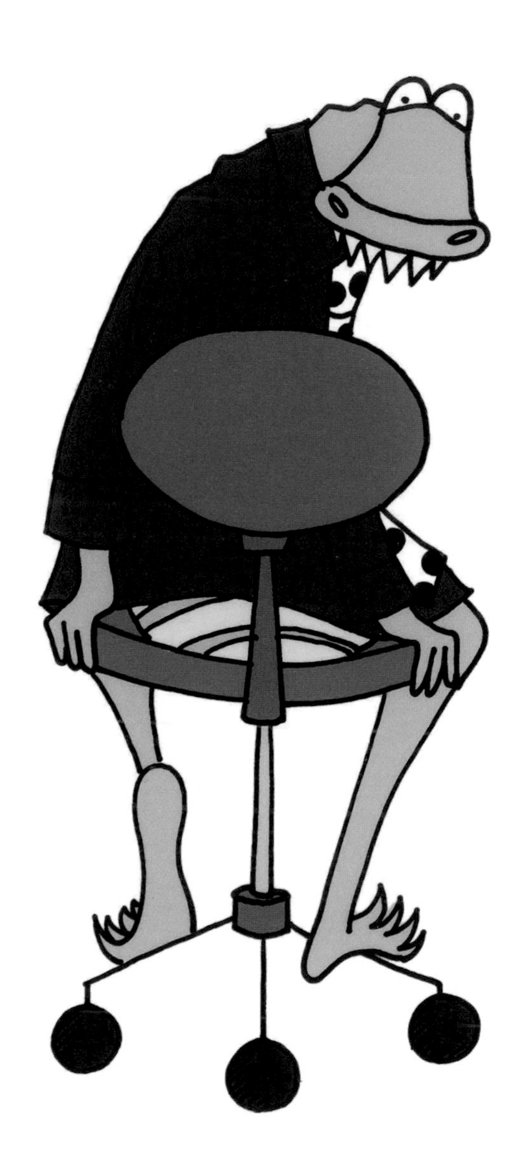

But it hurts to sit down . . . and it's uncomfortable walking home from work with his tail between his legs.

With your tail around your middle, you feel clumsy and it's easy to lose your balance.

One day, on his way home, crossing the road behind the Royal Palace,
John Jensen trips over the curb and falls head over heels onto the sidewalk.

Everyone stops and looks down at him.
They stand and stare.

John Jensen crawls to his feet. Everything hurts, but most of all his tail. He thinks it is badly bruised.

"You'll have to go to the doctor," a lady says.

A taxi takes John Jensen to the emergency room. He sits in the back seat crying. Big tears run down his cheeks and soak his tie.

At the Oslo hospital there's a man sitting behind a desk.

"What's wrong?" he asks.

"I fell and bruised my tail," John Jensen says.

"Take a number and wait in line," the man says.

John Jensen sits down with the others. You see strange things in an emergency room.

An elderly lady falls out of her chair and doesn't get up from the floor.

"She's fainted!" someone shouts.

"Is it her heart?" someone else asks.

People crowd around her, but they don't know how to help.

Suddenly John Jensen hears someone snorting through his nose. It sounds like a trumpet blast. A strong voice says, "Let me through; I'm a doctor!"

A huge figure in a white doctor's coat makes his way through the crowd. He has a stethoscope around his neck. It's Dr. Field.

He bends over the little lady, listens to her chest through the stethoscope, then lifts her up and carries her to one of the examination rooms.

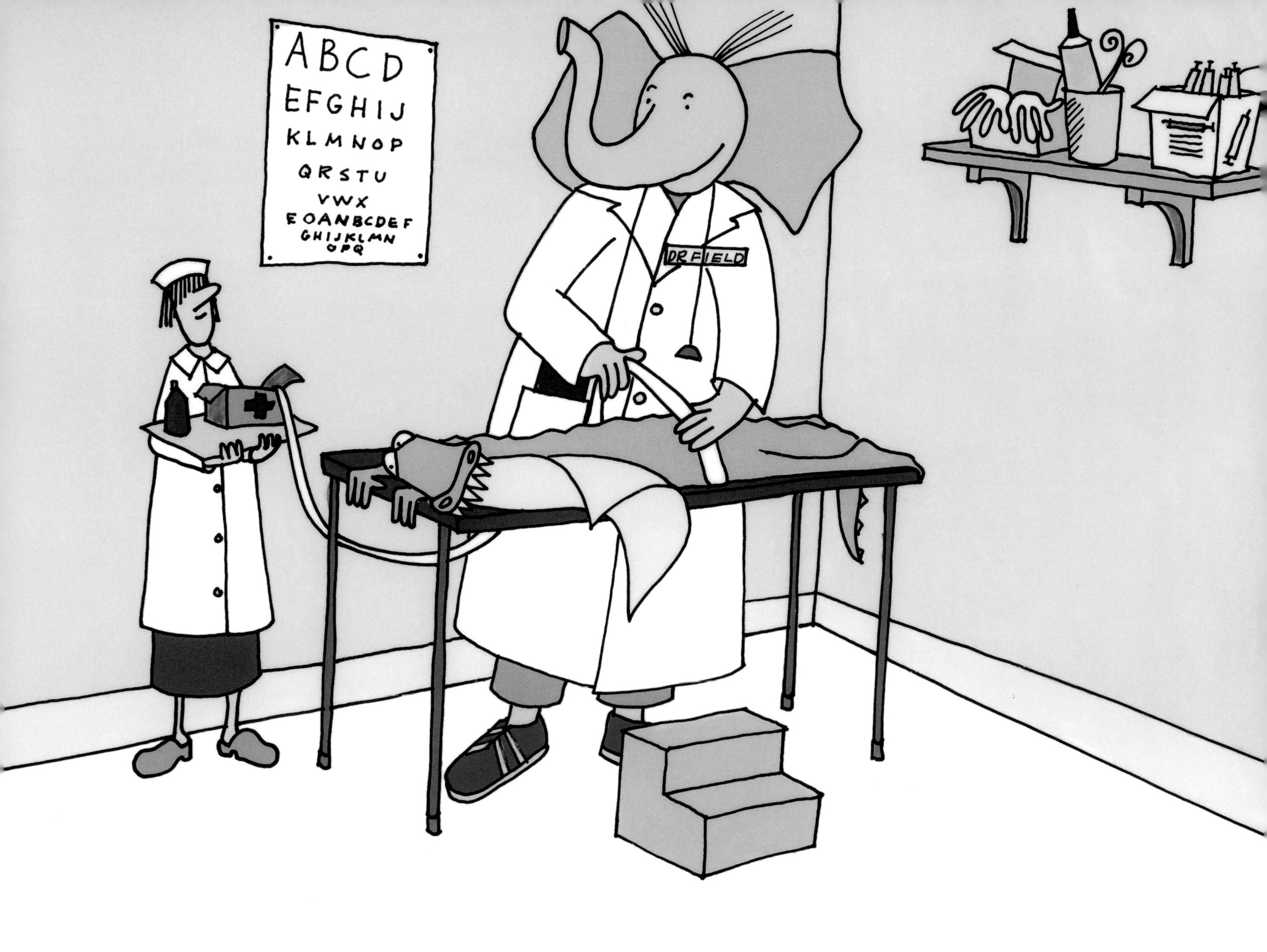

The wait at the hospital is rather long, but finally it's John Jensen's turn.
Dr. Field bandages his tail and listens to his chest and back through his stethoscope.

Dr. Field asks John Jensen to open his mouth
and say “Ahh” while he looks down his throat.

“Why did you tie up your tail?” Dr. Field asks.

“No one else has a tail like mine,”
John Jensen answers.

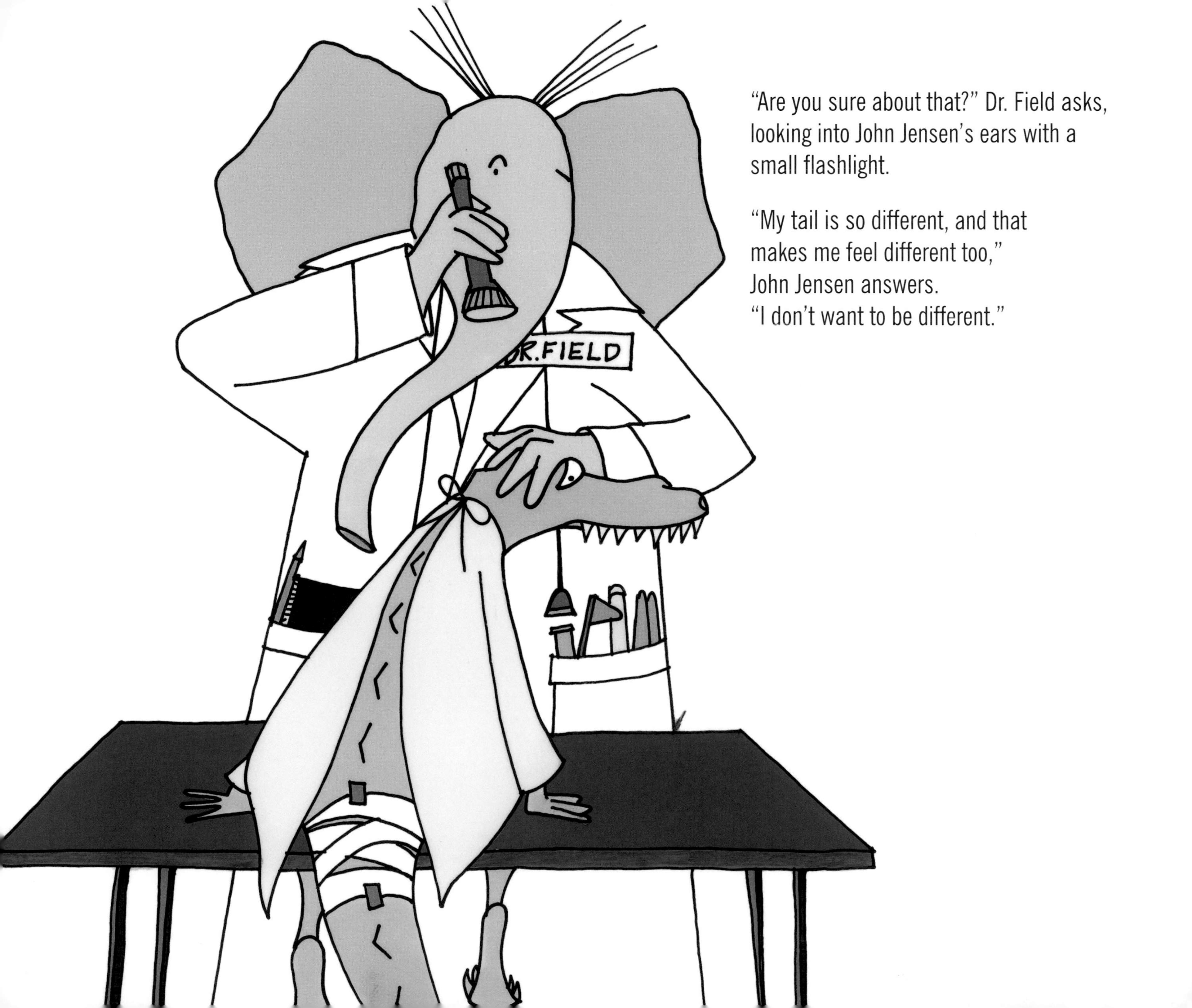

"Are you sure about that?" Dr. Field asks, looking into John Jensen's ears with a small flashlight.

"My tail is so different, and that makes me feel different too," John Jensen answers. "I don't want to be different."

"Some have tails, and some don't," Dr. Field says. "Some are like this, and some are like that. No two are exactly the same. Take me, for example. I have quite big ears."

. . . and a big nose, John Jensen thinks. He doesn't say so out loud. He just thinks it to himself.

“Big ears can be quite handy,” Dr. Field explains. “If you’re watching a scary movie, you can cover your eyes with them. I’m sure a tail is great too, if you think about it.”

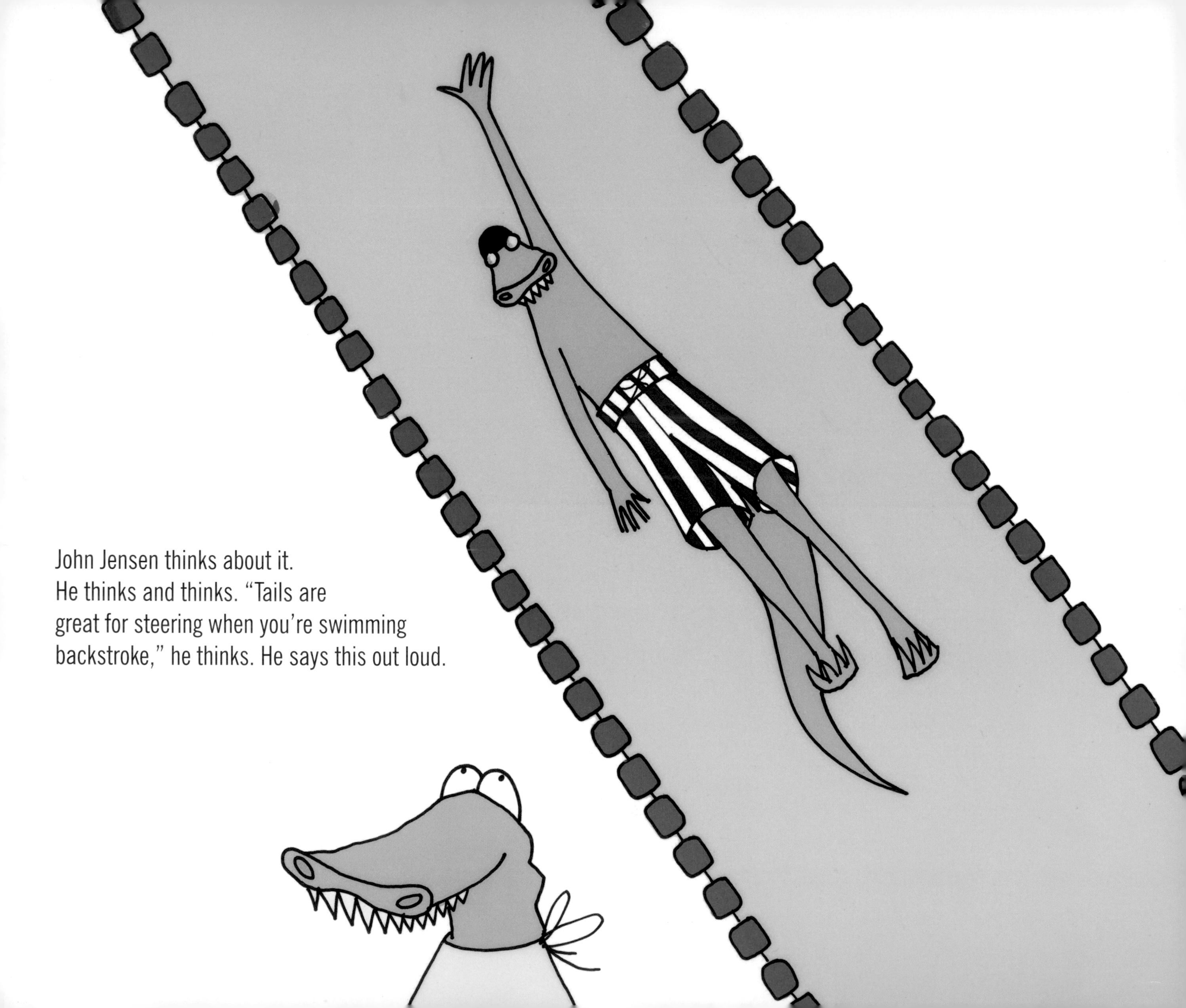

John Jensen thinks about it.
He thinks and thinks. “Tails are
great for steering when you’re swimming
backstroke,” he thinks. He says this out loud.

"Tails are great for stopping the ball when you're the goalie."

"Tails are great for keeping your balance when you're skating."

"Tails are great for tying bows to."

"Exactly," says Dr. Field. "Anyone who wears a bow is not afraid of being different."

"Exactly," says John Jensen.
"Anyone who wears a bow is not afraid."

It's the 17th of May, Norway's Constitution Day, and John Jensen is standing in front of the Royal Palace. He's wearing his best clothes, and he has a 17th of May bow tied around his tail. He still feels he's different. But that is just fine. He waves to the king, and the king waves back.